Sept. 2012

P9-BZQ-859

3 1488 0057U UUJ9

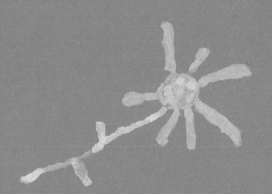

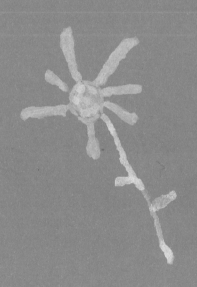

Algonquin Area Public Library
2600 Harnish Dr.
Algonquin, IL 60102
www.aapld.org

For Tim

PHILOMEL BOOKS
A division of Penguin Young Readers Group.   Published by The Penguin Group.
Penguin Group (USA) Inc., 375 Hudson Street, New York, NY 10014, U.S.A.
Penguin Group (Canada), 90 Eglinton Avenue East, Suite 700, Toronto, Ontario M4P 2Y3, Canada
(a division of Pearson Penguin Canada Inc.).
Penguin Books Ltd, 80 Strand, London WC2R 0RL, England.
Penguin Ireland, 25 St. Stephen's Green, Dublin 2, Ireland (a division of Penguin Books Ltd).
Penguin Group (Australia), 250 Camberwell Road, Camberwell, Victoria 3124, Australia
(a division of Pearson Australia Group Pty Ltd).
Penguin Books India Pvt Ltd, 11 Community Centre, Panchsheel Park, New Delhi - 110 017, India.
Penguin Group (NZ), 67 Apollo Drive, Rosedale, Auckland 0632, New Zealand
(a division of Pearson New Zealand Ltd).
Penguin Books (South Africa) (Pty) Ltd, 24 Sturdee Avenue, Rosebank, Johannesburg 2196, South Africa.
Penguin Books Ltd, Registered Offices: 80 Strand, London WC2R 0RL, England.

Copyright © 2012 by Jane Manning. All rights reserved. This book, or parts thereof, may not be reproduced in any form without permission in writing from the publisher, Philomel Books, a division of Penguin Young Readers Group, 345 Hudson Street, New York, NY 10014. Philomel Books, Reg. U.S. Pat. & Tm. Off. The scanning, uploading and distribution of this book via the Internet or via any other means without the permission of the publisher is illegal and punishable by law. Please purchase only authorized electronic editions, and do not participate in or encourage electronic piracy of copyrighted materials. Your support of the author's rights is appreciated. The publisher does not have any control over and does not assume any responsibility for author or third-party websites or their content.

Published simultaneously in Canada.   Manufactured in China by South China Printing Co. Ltd.

Edited by Jill Santopolo.   Design by Semadar Megged.   Text set in 15-point Alinea Incise.
The art was created by using Winsor & Newton watercolors on Lanaquarelle watercolor paper.

Library of Congress Cataloging-in-Publication Data
Manning, Jane.   Millie Fierce / Jane Manning.   p. cm.
Summary: Tired of being overlooked, Millie takes on a loud and obnoxious personality, which makes people notice her—for a little while.   [1. Behavior—Fiction. 2. Self-acceptance—Fiction.] I. Title.
PZ7.M31561Mi 2012   [E]—dc23   2011016347

ISBN 978-0-399-25642-4
1 3 5 7 9 10 8 6 4 2

Milllie Fierce

Jane Manning

PHILOMEL BOOKS
An Imprint of Penguin Group (USA) Inc.

Millie was too short to be tall,
too quiet to be loud,
and too plain to be fancy.

When she spoke at show-and-tell,
hardly anyone listened.
When she walked into a room,
hardly anyone looked up.

And when there was cake
to dish out,
Millie never got anything better
than a small, simple piece.

One day, Millie was drawing sidewalk pictures.
She had just finished a flower.
It was a little bit crooked,
but it was the best flower
she had ever drawn.

All at once,
three girls from school marched past her
as if she wasn't there.
They walked all over her flower,
    and over it,
        and over it,
until it was nothing more than a big,
multicolored smudge.

Millie sat there long after the girls had passed.

She looked at the smudge.

"That's me," she said.

Millie was tired of feeling like a smudge.

She didn't like it.

Not one bit.

A new feeling rumbled inside her.
Millie stood.
"I'm not a smudge," she said,
so loudly it surprised her.

That's when Millie became fierce.

Millie frizzed out her hair
and made the crazy eye.

She looked in the mirror and growled.

"Look at me and my ferocity!" she yelled.

Grandpa Edwin noticed.

She stomped around in Grandpa's noisy boots,
even though it made her toes tingle.
And she filed each of her nails to a tiny point.
"They are short, but they are sharp," she said.

She **scratched** them slowly
down the chalkboard.

The class noticed.

For Millie Fierce,
no line was too long to barge in front of,
no food was too tasty
to flick across the table.

Now people looked Millie Fierce right in the eye.
They were mad,
and said "SHHHH!" with angry faces,
but they noticed her.

She left muddy handprints on the
kitchen wall
and painted Buddy's face bright blue.

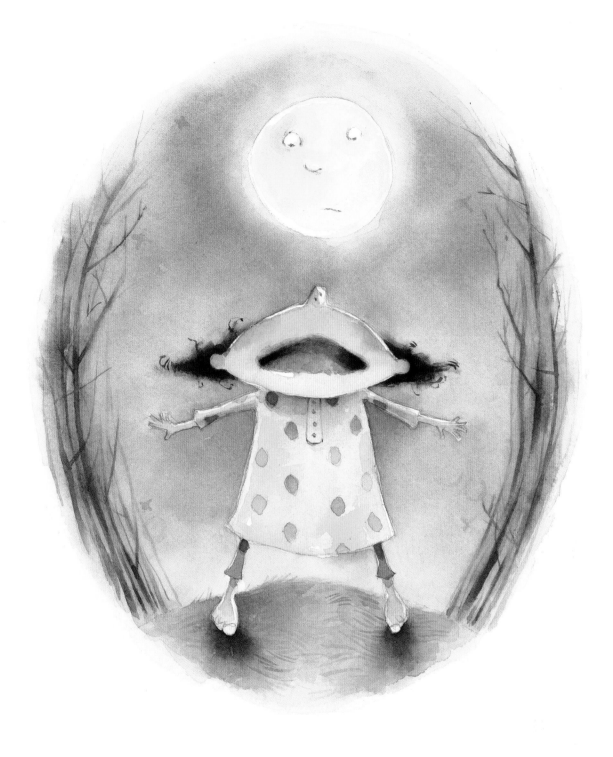

"Watch out! I bite!"
she howled like a mad thing.

The moon noticed.

Little by little,
people would sit farther and farther away from her.
Millie Fierce noticed that they didn't look at her as much.

So, she pulled all the buds off of Mrs. Klee's
favorite peony.
And laughed when Mrs. Klee's face turned beet red.
She only felt the littlest bit bad about it.

At school, during Jackie Raymond's birthday party,
Millie Fierce danced on her chair like a monkey,
but no one watched her,
not even to scowl.

So, Millie Fierce hid the tail of the donkey.
She dumped jelly beans on the floor.
"Just ignore her," said one of the girls in her class.
Everyone did.

So, Millie Fierce grabbed the biggest, best piece of cake,
the one with TWO roses on it.
She knew it was the birthday boy's piece.
She took it anyway.
Just before she took the first bite,
she looked around to see if anyone was watching her.
Everyone was.
But no one made a sound.

Except Jackie Raymond,
who was crying.

Millie Fierce hung her wild head.
For the first time in her life,
she wished she was invisible.

That day, Millie walked the
long way home.

She went up to her room and combed out her hair
and filed down her nails.
She drew a card for Jackie Raymond
with a flower on the outside.
"I'm sorry and Happy Birthday," she wrote on the inside,
and signed it "Millie."

She spit shined Grandpa's boots
and fed Buddy his supper.

Everyone noticed.

Millie decided she liked being good
better than being fierce.

Mostly.

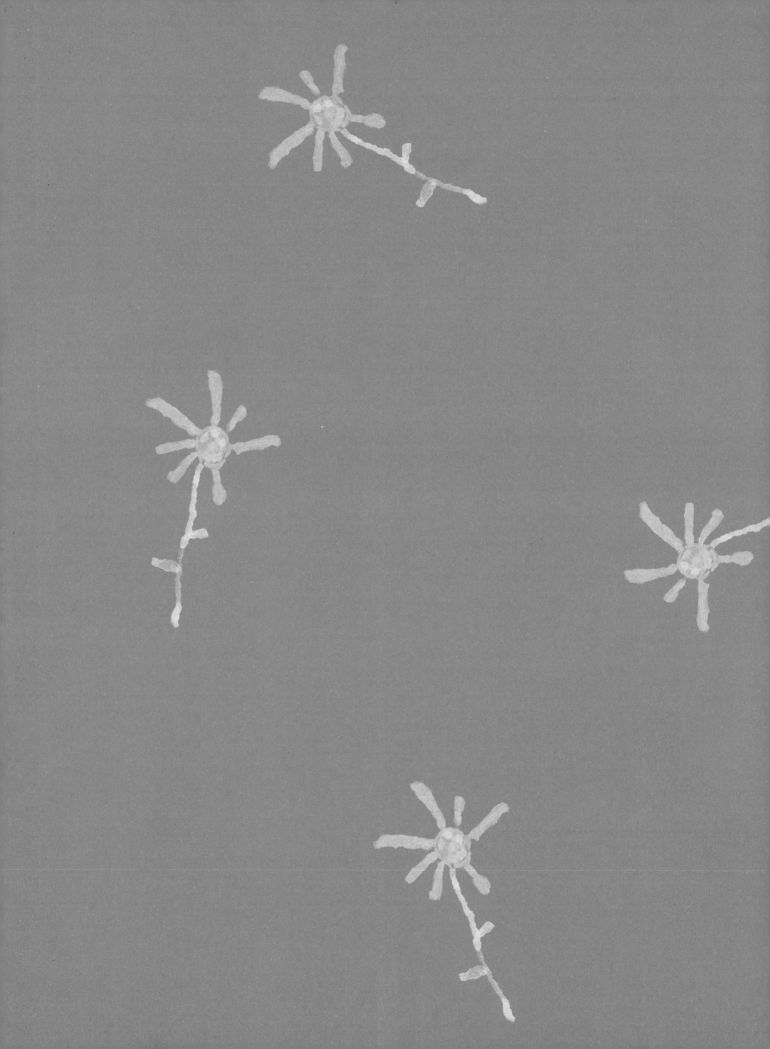